Cabbage Patch Kids

Three's a Crowd

by Jordan Horowitz   Illustrated by Cristina Ong

ISBN 0-590-45459-5

12 11 10 9 8 7 6 5 4 3 2   2 3 4 5 6 7/9

Printed in the U.S.A.   24

First Scholastic printing, August 1992

SCHOLASTIC INC.
New York Toronto London Auckland Sydney

Patricia Louise and Violetta Karbel did everything together.

They went for walks together.

They played games of hopscotch together.

They even held all their make-believe tea parties together.

They were like two peas in a pod. Or in this case, two cabbages in a patch.

One day Patricia Louise and Violetta Karbel
passed by the apple orchard. There they saw
Peter Thomas near one of the apple trees,
playing with a slingshot.

They watched as he raised his slingshot and
shot a pebble at the tree.

PING!

An apple fell right into his hand.

Patricia Louise had never played such a game. And on top of that, she was very hungry. As Peter Thomas bit into his juicy apple, she thought it would be fun to get one for herself.

"Bet I can hit one," said Patricia Louise.
"Girls don't know how to use a slingshot," laughed Peter Thomas.

Patricia Louise knew she could hit apples with a slingshot as well as any boy.

So taking the slingshot, she aimed and fired — but missed!

Peter Thomas laughed and laughed at Patricia Louise.

"I'll get one next time!" Patricia Louise said angrily.

"Yes, she'll get one next time," echoed Violetta Karbel.

Then Patricia Louise raised the slingshot and tried again.

PING!

This time she hit an apple so hard that it broke from the tree and fell on Peter Thomas's head. THUMP!

Now it was the girls' turn to laugh.

Soon Patricia Louise and Peter Thomas were laughing and eating all the ripe apples they could hit.

But now Violetta Karbel wasn't happy at all. She didn't want to play with the slingshot anymore. Patricia Louise is supposed to be *my* friend, she thought.

Violetta Karbel walked away.

Patricia Louise and Peter Thomas were
having too much fun to notice.

When they had eaten all the apples their
tummies could hold, they made a plan to meet
again tomorrow.

The next day Patricia Louise and Violetta Karbel had planned to play a game of house and have a tea party. It was Violetta Karbel's favorite game.

But today Patricia Louise wanted to play with Peter Thomas.

"Why don't you come with us?" Patricia Louise asked.

"I don't want to go," said Violetta Karbel. "I want to play house and have a party."

Besides, she didn't want to share her friend with anybody.

"Well, *I'm* going to play with Peter Thomas anyway," said Patricia Louise.

And off she went.

Violetta Karbel was all alone. She tried to play by herself. It wasn't very much fun.

Maybe I should have gone with Patricia Louise after all, she thought. So she decided to look for her.

She looked around the lake.

She looked around the boysenberry bushes.

She even looked around the smelly swamp.

She had just about given up looking when
she heard giggling from the apple orchard.

It was Patricia Louise and Peter Thomas.
They had a basket full of apples and were
eating them just as fast as they could.

They looked as if they didn't need her at all.

Patricia Louise and Peter Thomas are probably glad I didn't go along, thought Violetta Karbel angrily.

So she decided to play a trick on them.

That will ruin their picnic, she thought. Then Patricia Louise will be *my* best friend again.

So when they weren't looking, Violetta Karbel
sneaked something into their apple basket.
Then she hid behind the apple tree and
watched.

The next time Patricia Louise and Peter
Thomas put their hands in the apple basket, a
big slimy frog jumped out! It was a smelly,
muddy frog from the smelly, muddy swamp!
Patricia Louise didn't want to eat the apples
anymore.

They heard giggles from behind the apple
tree. It was Violetta Karbel.

"Violetta Karbel, you ruined our fun!" said
Patricia Louise angrily.

But Violetta Karbel just laughed and laughed.

Patricia Louise was so embarrassed that she ran away from the apple orchard.

Violetta Karbel was happy. She thought she had ruined Patricia Louise and Peter Thomas's picnic.

Then she heard someone laughing. It was Peter Thomas!

"What's so funny?" asked Violetta Karbel.

"That was a good trick!" replied Peter Thomas.

"I think you're silly," said Violetta Karbel. "That frog ruined all your apples. Aren't you mad?"

"Of course not," he said. "I LIKE frogs! And it didn't really ruin the apples."

"But that frog came from the smelly swamp," Violetta Karbel insisted.

"So?" Peter Thomas said. "The swamp is my all-time favorite place to play. But Patricia Louise won't ever go there. I guess girls are afraid of swamps."

"Not me," said Violetta Karbel. "I like the swamp."

So Violetta Karbel and Peter Thomas went
down to the swamp to play.

They caught frogs…
and toads…
and dragonflies….

They ran and jumped. They even played
hide-and-seek.

They had a great time.

Peter Thomas is lots of fun, Violetta Karbel thought. She felt silly for being mad at Patricia Louise.

Violetta Karbel decided to apologize to Patricia Louise.

But she decided to catch another dragonfly first.

Later that day Violetta Karbel found Patricia
Louise sitting at a picnic table.

"Patricia Louise," she said, "I have to talk
to you."

But Patricia Louise had on her mad face.

She got up and walked away from Violetta
Karbel.

Every day Violetta Karbel tried to apologize to Patricia Louise.

But every time she tried, Patricia Louise would make her mad face and walk away.

Finally, one day, Violetta Karbel and Patricia
Louise bumped into each other in the middle
of the narrowest road in the Cabbage Patch.

Neither girl could pass unless one of them
moved aside.

"I've got something to say to you, Patricia Louise," said Violetta Karbel. "And I won't let you pass until you listen. I'm sorry I played such a mean trick. And I want to be best friends again. Please."

But Patricia Louise was still mad at Violetta Karbel.

"I don't care what you say, Violetta Karbel. I'll never be your friend again."

Well, thought Violetta Karbel, if Patricia Louise can be mad at me, then I can be mad at her, too.

So both little girls stood in the narrow road and made mad faces at each other.

They squinted their eyes.
They stuck out their tongues.
They stretched their necks.
Soon both their faces became blue and red.

Suddenly they heard a sound coming from a ditch in
the side of the road.

SCRATCH! went the sound. SCRATCH! SCRATCH!

Violetta Karbel and Patricia Louise looked over at the
side of the road.

There in the ditch was Peter Thomas.

"What are you doing, Peter Thomas?" asked
Patricia Louise.

"Digging for worms!" said Peter Thomas.
"Want to help?"

Violetta Karbel and Patricia Louise looked at
each other with their mad faces.

"If she plays with you, I won't," said
Patricia Louise.

"I'll only play with you if she goes away,"
said Violetta Karbel.

Peter Thomas laughed and laughed.

"You won't play with me because you're girls. And everybody knows girls are afraid to dig for worms!"

Patricia Louise and Violetta Karbel looked at each other with their mad faces.

Suddenly their frowns changed into grins. Then their grins changed into smiles. Soon their mad faces had become happy.

"I'm glad we're friends again," said Patricia Louise. "That mad face was beginning to hurt!"

"Besides," said Violetta Karbel as they climbed down into the ditch together, "I know we can dig for worms as well as you can, Peter Thomas."

And they did.